Hop aboard this bus of stories f
for four year olds! You'll meet l
Poonam and her *most* unusual p
people; Mr Briggs, the amazing
unusual and exciting characters,

No story has been allowed on the bus without careful inspection
by children's book specialist Pat Thomson. All the stories are tried
and tested favourites for sharing with young children by top
children's authors – Joan Aiken, Ruth Ainsworth, John Cunliffe,
Helen Cresswell, Catherine Storr and many others.

PAT THOMSON is a well-known author and anthologist.
Additionally, she works as a lecturer and librarian in a teacher
training college – work which involves a constant search for short
stories which have both quality and child-appeal. She is also an
Honorary Vice-President of the Federation of Children's Book
Groups. She is married with two grown-up children and lives in
Northamptonshire.

Also available by Pat Thomson,
and published by Corgi Books:

A POCKETFUL OF STORIES FOR FIVE YEAR OLDS

A BUCKETFUL OF STORIES FOR SIX YEAR OLDS

A BASKET OF STORIES FOR SEVEN YEAR OLDS

A SACKFUL OF STORIES FOR EIGHT YEAR OLDS

A CHEST OF STORIES FOR NINE YEAR OLDS

A SATCHEL OF SCHOOL STORIES

A STOCKING FULL OF CHRISTMAS STORIES

A BUS

full of Stories for Four Year Olds

COLLECTED BY PAT THOMSON

Illustrated by Steve Cox

CORGI BOOKS

A BUS FULL OF STORIES FOR FOUR YEAR OLDS

A CORGI BOOK : 0 552 52816 1

First published in Great Britain by Doubleday,
a division of Transworld Publishers Ltd

PRINTING HISTORY
Doubleday edition published 1994
Corgi edition published 1995

Collection copyright © 1994 Pat Thomson
Illustrations © 1994 Steve Cox

The right of Pat Thomson to be identified as the Author
of this work has been asserted in accordance with the
Copyright Designs and Patents Act 1988.

Corgi Books are published by Transworld Publishers Ltd,
61–63 Uxbridge Road, Ealing, London W5 5SA,
in Australia by Transworld Publishers (Australia) Pty Ltd,
15–25 Helles Avenue, Moorebank, NSW 2170,
and in New Zealand by Transworld Publishers (NZ) Ltd,
3 William Pickering Drive, Albany, Auckland.

Printed and bound in Great Britain by
Cox & Wyman Ltd, Reading, Berkshire

CONTENTS

Yanni

I will tell you a story about Yanni.

Yanni was walking along a lonely road to visit his sweetheart. And as he passed by a fountain, a dragon sprang out from behind it.

Said the dragon, 'Good morning, good morning, my Yanni, my dinner!'

Yanni trembled and said, 'Good morning, my dragon! Oh please do not eat me!'

But the dragon said, 'I am hungry, my Yanni, I am hungry, my dinner!'

Said Yanni, 'My dragon, my dragon, if your dinner I must be, let me first say goodbye to my dear little sweetheart.'

Yanni

Said the dragon, 'You shall go on your way to your sweetheart, my Yanni. You shall bid her goodbye for ever and ever, if you swear to come back, for I must have my dinner!'

So Yanni swore he would come back, and he went sadly on his way, and came to the house of his little sweetheart.

Said his little sweetheart, 'Why are you sad, my Yanni, my lover? Do I no longer please you, my Yanni?'

And Yanni said, 'Oh how greatly you please me, my dear little sweetheart! But a dragon I met by the fountain has asked me to dinner.'

Said his dear little· sweetheart, 'Where you go, Yanni, I will go with you.'

But Yanni said, 'Where I am going, no maid shall go with me.'

3

Said his little sweetheart, 'I will cook you a dinner, my Yanni, my lover. I will shake up your mattress, and spread out your blanket.'

But Yanni said, 'Where I am going, my dear little sweetheart, no maid shall go with me. There is no cooking, nor eating, nor spreading of mattress, nor sleeping in that place.'

And his little sweetheart said, 'Yet I will go with you, Yanni, my lover. Our love will protect us.'

So the two of them set out, like two pretty doves that fly into the fowler's net.

And there was the dragon leaning against the fountain.

When the dragon saw them walking towards him, he cried out, 'My dinner, my dinner! My dinner comes double!'

And when Yanni heard this, he said, 'Did I not tell you, my dear little sweetheart, that you should not have come here?'

But his dear little sweetheart said in a loud voice, 'Go on, go on, my Yanni, my lover! Go on, and fear not. *I have eaten nine dragons for breakfast – I will now eat the tenth one!*'

When the dragon heard this, he trembled and said, 'Pray tell me, friend Yanni, pray tell me, my dinner, whose daughter is that one?'

Then the dear little sweetheart stepped boldly in front of Yanni, and said, 'I am the daughter of Lightning, grand-daughter of Thunder. Move aside, Yanni. *I will flash with my lightning, I will crash with my thunder! I will eat this small dragon!*'

But the dragon flew off. He flew off in haste. And he never came back to eat up friend Yanni.

This story is by Ruth Manning-Sanders.

Alexander

Alexander was a new baby. He was so new that all his aunts and uncles and cousins came to see him. Mum unwrapped him, and they counted his ten toes and ten fingers, and said how tiny and pink they were. Everyone said, 'He's beautiful!'

Everyone, that is, except his big sister, Liselotte.

Liselotte didn't think Alexander was

beautiful at all. How could he be, when he had no teeth and hardly any hair? Besides that, he made wet and smelly messes in his nappy, and when he was hungry he screamed so loudly you could hear him all over the house.

Liselotte didn't wear nappies any more, even at night, and she wasn't allowed to scream. Even when she was hungry she had to say please and thank you. She had ten toes and ten fingers, like Alexander, but the aunts and uncles and cousins didn't say anything about that. They were too busy fussing over Alexander.

As soon as they went away, Liselotte said, 'I don't like Alexander. Can we put him back in your tummy?'

'No,' said Mum. 'Once a baby is born he can't go back. Alexander is your own little baby brother. You'll be able to play with him soon.'

'He's too tiny, and he's always asleep,' said Liselotte. 'I'd rather play with my doll.'

'He'll grow, and he'll wake up more,' said Mum. 'Why don't you give him a cuddle? Sit on the couch and I'll put him in your lap.'

'No, I don't want to,' said Liselotte.

She put her big doll in its pram, covered it with the red check blanket Grandma had knitted, and pushed the pram outside in the garden.

That night Alexander cried. Mum

changed his nappy and fed him, but he still cried. Dad walked up and down holding him, but he still cried. He was crying when Liselotte went to bed, and he was crying when she woke up. He had cried all night.

By the time the family sat down to breakfast he was screaming.

'I think you'd better sell that baby,' Dad said, as he went off to work.

'Good idea,' said Mum as she walked up and down rubbing Alexander's back.

Suddenly he gave a loud burp and in two minutes he was asleep.

Mum wrapped him up tightly in a bunny rug and put him in a basket in Liselotte's room.

'I'm worn out!' she said. 'Liselotte, you play quietly for a while and let me rest.'

She lay on the bed and in two minutes she was asleep, too.

Liselotte went to the basket and looked at Alexander. He was so tightly wrapped up that she could only see one round pink cheek and a small nose like a button.

If I could sell him, she thought, Mum wouldn't have to stay up all night.

Alexander was about the same size as Liselotte's doll, so she had no trouble lifting him out of the basket, bundle and all, and putting him in her doll's pram. She covered him with the red check blanket, and wheeled him outside and down the street.

Her friend the postman came along on his bike.

'Hello,' said Liselotte. 'Do you want to buy a baby?'

The postman looked at the bundle in the pram and thought it was Liselotte's doll.

'No thank you. I've got two of my own at home. That's quite enough for me.'

Liselotte went a little further and saw her friend Mrs Smith.

'Hello, Mrs Smith,' she said. 'Do you want to buy a baby?'

'Not today, Liselotte,' said Mrs Smith with a smile. 'You won't cross the road, will you dear?'

If I can't cross the road, Liselotte thought, how can I go to the shops to sell the baby?

Just then she saw her friend Oscar riding his tricycle up and down his drive.

'Hello, Oscar. Do you want to buy a baby?'

'Is it a girl baby or a boy baby?' asked Oscar.

'It's a baby brother.'

'Hm, I'd like one of those,' said Oscar.

'How much money have you got?' asked Liselotte.

'None,' said Oscar, 'but I'll swap him for my teddy.'

'All right,' said Liselotte. So she wheeled her doll's pram into Oscar's house, and lifted Alexander on to the couch. He was still asleep.

Oscar found his teddy under his bunk and gave it to Liselotte. She examined the teddy very carefully, the way the aunts and uncles and cousins had looked at Alexander.

'His fur's all nasty,' she said.

'That's because he fell in the bath one night,' said Oscar.

16

'One of his ears is coming off,' said Liselotte.

'He's nearly as old as I am,' said Oscar. 'Your mum can sew it on.'

'He hasn't got ten toes and ten fingers, like Alexander.'

'That's because he's a teddy.'

'Well, I like Alexander better than your teddy,' said Liselotte.

'You can't change back,' said Oscar.

'Yes I can.'

'You can't have him.'

'I can *so*!' said Liselotte, throwing the teddy on the floor. She went to get Alexander, but Oscar stood in front of the couch.

'Move away! I want my baby brother! He's mine!' Liselotte shouted.

She shouted so loudly that Oscar's mum came running in to see what was wrong.

'Liselotte! Does your mother know you're here?' She saw the bundle on the couch and lifted the bunny rug from Alexander's face. She gave a little scream. 'Liselotte! Did you bring that baby here?'

'My mum and dad want to sell him,' said Liselotte.

'What nonsense! Come home with me at once. Your mother must be out of her mind with worry.' And she

18

scooped up Alexander and scurried along the street with Liselotte running behind, pushing her doll's pram, and Oscar chasing them on his tricycle. Teddy was left behind on the floor.

Liselotte's mum had just woken up, found the empty basket, and dashed out into the street. There she saw Oscar's mum clutching the baby, Liselotte running along behind with the pram, and Oscar pedalling hard on his tricycle.

'You naughty girl, Liselotte!' she said, grabbing Alexander. 'Why on earth did you take him?'

Alexander was still asleep.

'You said you wanted to sell him,' said Liselotte.

'Of course we wouldn't sell him!' said her mother. 'It was a joke!'

When they had all calmed down a

little, she said thank you to Oscar's mum for bringing the baby home, and she and Liselotte went inside the house where Mum tucked Alexander back in his basket.

'Liselotte,' she said, 'stop crying and listen to me. You must never *never* pick up Alexander without asking. He is so soft and tiny you could hurt him without meaning to.'

Liselotte said in a very small voice, 'Will you sell me, now you've got Alexander?'

'Never, never, *never!*' said Mum. 'You're our special little girl; the best in the whole world.' And she gave Liselotte a big hug.

'I didn't hurt him, did I?' asked Liselotte.

'No, he's all right, he didn't even know he was kidnapped. Come and see,' said Mum, and she unwrapped the bunny rug.

Alexander was just waking up. His blue stretch suit covered his toes, but he waved his fists, and Liselotte looked at his ten tiny pink fingers. He gave a huge yawn, and she saw his mouth without any teeth. Then he opened his eyes, and when he saw Liselotte bending over him his mouth stretched wide and this time he wasn't yawning.

'He's *smiling*!' said Liselotte's mum. 'His very first smile, and it's for you, Liselotte!'

Liselotte put her finger into Alexander's hand and his tiny fingers curled round and held it tight.

She said, 'He's beautiful!'

This story is by June Epstein.

The Bear Who Liked Hugging People

There was once a bear who lived in a cave in the mountains. He was a mountain bear. He ate fruit and berries and did no harm to anybody, but he had one bad habit. He *would* hug people. He only hugged them because he liked them, but they did not know that. His furry arms were so strong that he hugged much too tightly. Some of the people he hugged were never the same

23

again. They were quite flat when he let them go, and lop-sided.

Not many people went along the rough track that passed the door of his cave, but he never failed to rush at them, his arms outstretched, to give them a loving hug.

The people living near dared not pass that way or let their children go by alone. They used, instead, a very long, steep, rocky path that led them right up on the side of the mountain. It took much longer and was difficult to find at night or in the snow.

The mothers were particularly worried about their children, who emerged from the bear's hug quite a different shape, flat instead of round, with snub noses which completely changed their expression.

24

The men of the neighbourhood met together to decide what to do for the best. Should they catch the bear and put him in a cage in a zoo? Or should they shoot him and make something useful out of his fur, a coat or a rug? They decided, rather sadly, to shoot him, and the wife of the man who shot him should be given the skin for a fur coat. They were upset about this, but there seemed no other way out. They could not risk their little children being deformed and it did not seem as though the bear would change his habits.

About this time, a poor man who lived far away, on the other side of the mountain, decided to go and visit his old mother who lived down in the valley. He had saved downy goose feathers to make a deep, billowy feather bed to give her as a present. One day, he left home and travelled over the mountain with the new feather bed rolled up and strapped on his back.

When he got near the cave where the bear lived, the bear smelled him coming and came lumbering out into the sunshine, his furry arms outstretched.

26

The traveller remembered hearing stories of a bear who hugged people and he called out loudly:

'Lord Bear. I've brought you a present. I've brought you something warm and just made to be hugged. Wait while I unstrap it from my back.'

The bear waited, because he was a good-natured fellow, and when the bed was unstrapped, but still in a roll, he took it in his arms and gave it a tight, close hug.

It did not struggle or cry out. It melted into his arms with softness and warmth.

'Keep it,' said the traveller, shaking with fear. 'Keep it, my Lord. I made it for you.'

This was not really true as he had made it for his old mother, but a man may change his mind. And the bear did not know about the old mother.

So he kept it and carried it into his cave and hugged it every night, when he went to sleep. This satisfied him and he quite gave up hugging other people. The men in the neighbourhood gave

up the horrid idea of shooting him, too. Even the smallest children were now quite safe when passing his cave door alone.

All the cold, dark winter the bear dozed in his cave, under the snow, his feather bed held tightly in his arms.

When the spring came with the flowers and birds, he woke up and was lucky enough to meet with a wife, a young bear just old enough to get married. So if he felt like hugging anybody, she was always near at hand and loved to be hugged.

As for the feather bed, they kept it in the cave and slept on it. This was much more comfortable than lying on the hard, rocky floor.

This story is by Ruth Ainsworth.

The Magic Thistledown Dog

I want to tell you about an old man and woman who lived in a cottage near Matlock wood. The cottage was small, and they had not much money, but they were happy enough. The cottage was always clean and bright, and in the garden they grew potatoes and cabbages and beautiful lemon-coloured roses.

In the autumn, the man would go into the wood to pick blackberries and collect sticks for the fire. One day, he heard a tiny cry coming from between the roots of a huge old oak tree. And there, waving at him, was a pixie dressed in a green coat and green pointed hat. The hat had a bright red feather in it.

'Help, help,' cried the pixie. 'I am trapped between the roots of this oak tree. I can't climb over them and I can't squeeze under them. Will you come over here and lift me out, please?'

To reach the pixie, the man had to step through a patch of thistles that prickled his ankles above his shoes and made them very sore. He pressed and pressed aside the roots of the oak tree, gently lifted out the pixie, and dusted him down. Then he gave him first pick

of the bowl of blackberries he had been gathering. When the pixie had eaten his fill of one large blackberry, he thanked the man in his high, sing-song voice.

'Pixies make wishes come true for people who are kind to them,' he said. 'And you have been very kind to me, old man. Tell me your heart's desire and I will work magic for you.'

The man thought long and hard about the wish. He was tempted to ask the pixie to stop his ankles from hurting from the prickles, but he knew that at home, in the cupboard, was a jar of ointment which would work as well, if he were patient about it. He thought of asking for great wealth, but decided he was happier with his wife, in their little cottage.

'There is one thing my wife and I would like,' said the man to the pixie. 'We would like a little companion to walk with on summer days and cheer us up on winter evenings.'

When he had said this, the pixie took the red feather out of his hat and waved it over the patch of thistles. As it was autumn-time, some of the thistles were covered in that soft, white woolly stuff called thistledown. A ball of this thistledown grew and grew until, before the surprised eyes of the man, it turned into a fluffy little white dog, with a black nose and eyes as round and black as the berries the man was holding.

The little dog's tail shot up and curled over his back as tight as a corkscrew. He looked at the man with his blackberry eyes and bared his teeth into what was

35

most certainly a grin. Then he gave a bark, stood up on his back legs and plunged off into the undergrowth.

'Don't go! Come back here!' shouted the man, and he followed the little dog with never a thought for the pixie.

When they arrived home the man's wife was working at her wooden spinning-wheel, spinning loose wool into yarn for a neighbouring farmer. When she saw the little dog, she stopped spinning at once.

'Why, what have we here?' she cried. 'Are you a little dog or a little lamb or what?'

She bent down and hugged the little fellow, then hurried to the kitchen to find him something to eat.

From that day, the little dog stayed with the old man and woman and they were all very happy together. The man and woman fed him well, and in return the little dog guarded the house. He went for walks through the wood with them, and played with the squirrels and rabbits. And at night, when they all sat together around a crackling log fire, the little dog would roll over with a sigh of contentment, stick his legs in the air, show his tummy and grin.

'He really has the most wonderful white wool,' said the woman, stroking him. 'Far better than any of the sheep's wool the farmer gives me to spin. And look how it's growing. We never need fear that our little white dog will feel the cold winter winds.'

But spring came early that year, with a sudden warm spell that brought out the celandines and bluebells, and even a bumble-bee or two. The little dog was feeling very hot in his woolly coat, so, while the man held him still, the woman took up a pair of long, sharp scissors and snip-snipped, ever so gently, at the soft white wool which floated to the floor like finest thistle-down.

The strange thing was, the more she snipped, the more the wool seemed to grow. Soon the room was full of it – like soft, floating clouds. Only when the man and woman had packed it all into a bag, and filled the bag many times over, did the little dog's wool stop growing – and he looked a bit like a shorn sheep. Then he started to frolic about, and show how pleased he was. And a little bird who had perched on the windowsill caught a piece of the wool in her beak and flew off to line her nest with it.

The man washed all the wool from the little white dog, and spread it to dry in the sunshine. And that evening, instead of spinning wool from the farmer's sheep, the woman started to spin the little dog's wool. She worked night after night and soon had piles of the softest, whitest yarn.

By the time winter came round again, she had knitted the yarn into the most beautiful coverlet that had ever been seen in that part of the country. The man and woman put the coverlet on their bed and found it warmer than toast and lighter than a feather. All their neighbours came to admire it, and the little white dog lay down on top of it and snored.

But there was one man in the village who not only admired the coverlet, but wanted one for himself. This man was called Bad Jem, and he lived on an acre of land in a broken-down caravan.

Bad Jem was not kind to animals. He set a rabbit-trap in the wood, and one dark night he stepped into it, which everyone said was justice. He tried keeping hens, but fed them so badly they all ran away. And it was this Jem who lay in wait in the wood for the little white dog, threw an old blanket over him and carried him off to a hut, which no-one knew was there, on the acre of land at the back of his caravan.

There was one small window in the hut, high up and dirty, and very little light came through. The air in the hut was cold and damp. Bad Jem tied the little white dog to a post in a corner and gave him only a heap of filthy straw to sleep on. He tossed him scraps of bone and gristle and more often than not forgot to fill his water dish. The little dog thought of the old man and woman, and how they would be missing him, and tears trickled from his deep, soulful blackberry eyes down to his blackberry nose. But still the spell kept working and his coat kept growing – and there was a reason for this, as you will see.

The old man and woman were heartbroken at losing their little companion. They combed the countryside in search of him and hung notices on the trees promising rewards for his return. But they did not once think of Bad Jem and his acre of land behind the broken-down caravan.

Weeks passed, and Bad Jem went to the village shop and bought himself a pair of the longest, sharpest scissors. He shouted at the little white dog as he cut and hacked at the wool. The little dog stood very still, for he knew Jem would poke his eye out as soon as look at him.

Soon the hut was filled with floating clouds of softest wool, as the old couple's room had been. Bad Jem jumped for joy.

'I will keep you for ever,' he told the little white dog. 'And I will make coverlets to sell every week at the market. Soon I will be a rich man.'

The little dog's tail, which had not curled like a corkscrew since the day Bad Jem made off with him, now disappeared completely between his back legs and looked as if it would never come up again.

Bad Jem collected together all the wool but, being Jem, he did not think of washing it. He carried a broken-down old spinning-wheel into the hut and tried to spin the wool, but the first thing he did was to prick his finger.

There are some people who, when misfortune hits them, have to make others unhappy too – and Jem was one of those people. Hopping about with pain he picked up a big stick and was just about to hit the little dog with it when there was a flash of green up at the tiny window. Jem turned in amazement to see the pixie sitting there.

'Drop that stick,' ordered the pixie. 'Or I will turn you into a jelly baby.'

Jem dropped the stick at once.

'I ought to turn you into one anyway,' continued the pixie. 'This little dog is a friend of mine and you have treated him shamefully. But if you make amends, and set him free, I will wave the feather from my hat and turn the pile of wool you are sitting on into a wonderful coverlet. I can't say fairer than that, can I?'

Jem shook his head, thinking secretly

45

that he could always kidnap the little dog again, when the pixie was far away. He untied the rope from the little white dog's neck and the little dog stretched his legs painfully and hobbled to the door. Then he started to run across the field, getting stronger and stronger, until he reached the cottage where his two old friends lived.

How they cried with joy to see him, and patted him and hugged him, I hardly need to tell you. The little white dog had the best meal of his life that evening – tasty meat stew with cabbage and herbs, special biscuits and a dish of pure spring water. Then he went upstairs and stretched out on the wool coverlet and snored happily. The old man and woman crept into bed and snored happily too.

And what of Bad Jem?

Back at his broken-down caravan he, too, was planning to step inside a coverlet – the wonderful wool coverlet which had appeared when the pixie waved his feather over the pile of the little dog's wool. And, except for the old couple's coverlet, it was the softest, lightest one in the world for, as you will have guessed by now, the little white dog was a magic dog and his wool was not really wool but the softest thistle-down.

And so it was with the greatest antici-pation that Bad Jem threw off all his clothes and climbed into bed and snuggled down under the coverlet.

But as soon as he did so, the thistle-down turned back into *thistles* – the prickliest, deadliest thistles imaginable.

'Ow! . . . Ooh! . . . Ahh! . . . Help!
. . . Save me!' cried Bad Jem.

But though he shouted and struggled
and kicked, no-one heard him. And the
more he struggled and kicked the more
he became entangled with the prickles.

48

And the more they pricked his arms and legs and buttocks, until they were red raw, the louder he yelled.

And he never *ever*, tried to steal the little white dog again.

This story is by Wendy Eyton.

Tom

When Tom was a very small boy, his grandmothers and grandfathers and his aunts and uncles and cousins used to look at him and say,

'He has the family nose. It is just like Jack's and his grandpa's.'

'He has hair like Aunt Em's.'

'His eyes are exactly like mine,' said one of his grandmas.

'And his chin is like my brother's, his

great Uncle Harry,' said a grandpa.

'He has ears just like his cousin Paul's,' said an aunt.

'When he scowls he reminds me of old cousin Wilfred. I wonder if he will have a temper like that,' said an uncle.

While Tom was quite small he didn't mind this sort of talk. But when he grew older he didn't like it all.

'Why do my eyes and my ears and my nose and my hair have to be like anyone else's? Why can't I just be me, Tom?' he asked.

He decided to show everyone that he was different from everyone else. He would do some extraordinary things. Tom stood on his head for five whole minutes and waved his legs in the air.

But his grandma said, 'Look! That's just what his Uncle Jack used to do.'

SO THAT WAS NO GOOD.

Tom took off his clothes and painted himself green all over.

But his Aunt Em said, 'I remember Tom's dad doing that. Only he painted himself blue, not green.'

SO THAT WAS NO GOOD.

Tom jumped up and down forty-seven times and shouted, 'Down with jelly babies!'

And his Uncle Peter said, 'Funny! That's what I used to do when I was fed up with everyone around me.'

SO THAT WAS NO GOOD.

At last Tom was so tired of his family that he decided to run away to find somewhere where no-one would say 'Isn't Tom like . . . his grandpa . . . his aunt . . . his uncle . . . his cousin.'

He walked out of his house and he walked and he walked and he walked. He walked a very long way, and he became very tired. When he stopped walking he was in a street he had never seen before. All the houses were strange and so were all the people. Suddenly Tom knew that he was very hungry as well as tired. He was missing his mum and his dad and he wished he had never run away so far from home. He tried to remember the way he had come so that he could go back. But he couldn't remember properly and soon he was more lost than ever.

Tom asked several people who passed him in the street, 'Can you tell me how to get back to my house in Park Road?' But no-one could tell him. He felt very sad and he did not know what to do next. But suddenly he saw a large red bus with the number seven written on its front.

'Aha! The Number Seven bus goes near my street,' Tom thought, and he began to walk in the direction in which the bus was going.

Presently, as he walked, Tom heard the sound of a long, slow hoot.

'That is the hooter of one of the boats that sails on the canal near where I live,' Tom thought, and he walked faster.

Then Tom smelled the smell of delicious new bread.

'I know that smell! It is the smell of

56

the new bread that is baked every morning by Mr Georgias in his shop on the corner of my street,' thought Tom, and he began to run, following the delicious smell. Almost at once he saw Mr Georgias's shop, and the moment after he saw his mum standing on the step of the house where he lived, looking anxiously up and down the street.

'Tom! Where have you been? I've been looking for you everywhere,' she said as she hugged him.

So Tom explained that he had run away because he was so tired of everyone saying that how he looked and what he did were just like how the rest of the family looked and what the rest of the family did.

'But I found my way back from ever so far away by seeing the Number Seven bus with my own eyes. And I heard the canal boat's hooter with my own ears and I smelled Mr Georgias's delicious new bread with my own nose. So now I know that they are really mine and don't belong to anyone else. So I shan't have to run away again,' said Tom.

This story is by Catherine Storr.

Farmer Barnes and Bluebell

It was autumn and Farmer Barnes was busy sawing logs.

Little John ran into the yard, shouting, 'She's gone! She's gone! She's gone!'

Farmer Barnes stopped sawing and said, 'Who? What? Where?'

His wife Emily came out, wiping her hands on her apron.

Baby Candy sat up in her pram and opened her eyes very wide.

They all looked at little John and he said, '*Bluebell!*'

Farmer Barnes said not another word. He left the saw in the wood. He put on his jacket. He ran to the north meadow where the cows were grazing. He counted them on his fingers – 'Two . . . four . . . six. Three under the tree. Four at the trough. Four by the barn. Seventeen all together! One missing! It *is* Bluebell! She's run away again! Oh, deary me, *where* has she gone? I must find her before she gets into trouble!'

He ran across the meadow and into the lane. Bluebell was not to be seen, so Farmer Barnes ran down the lane towards the village.

He had not gone very far when he

met Miss Smith. She was leaning against a gate, dabbing her face with a white lace handkerchief.

Farmer Barnes called out to her, 'Good day to you, Miss Smith! Have you seen my Bluebell? She's run away and I cannot find her!'

'I have *not* seen your Bluebell,' said Miss Smith, 'but a bull chased me all down the lane! I had to jump over the gate to get away! At *my* age too! I was

wearing my second-best hat, the one with cherries on it, and it fell in the mud. The foolish beast tried to eat the cherries, then tossed the hat in the air and ran down the lane, so it was Goodbye bull and Goodbye hat, too!'

'Dear me, what a business!' said Farmer Barnes. 'Who would let a bull out? And it ran towards the village? What next? If I don't catch her . . .' Then Farmer Barnes went quickly down the lane.

He had not gone very far when he met Farmer Grey. He was standing by a broken fence, looking very angry.

Farmer Barnes called out to him, 'Have you seen my Bluebell? She's run away and I cannot find her!'

'I have *not* seen your Bluebell,' said Farmer Grey, 'but someone has broken

my new fence down and eaten my best apples!'

'Dear me, what a business!' said Farmer Barnes. 'Who would do that? Perhaps the boy from the village? Who knows?' He hurried down the lane before Farmer Grey could say another word.

Farmer Barnes had not gone very far when he met Mr Trench. He was standing outside his house looking very sad. There was a table by his gate, with a notice saying:

On the table were three empty baskets, and six baskets upside down. Squashed plums were everywhere; plums on the grass, plums in the road, in hundreds and hundreds!

Farmer Barnes called out to Mr Trench, 'Have you seen my Bluebell? She's run away and I cannot find her!'

'I have *not* seen your Bluebell,' said Mr Trench, 'but see what someone has done to my lovely plums! All spoilt! Such a mess! What shall I do? Oh dear! Oh dear!' He took out a small blue handkerchief and wiped his eyes.

'Dear me, what a business!' said Farmer Barnes. 'Who would do that? Perhaps the crows? Who knows?' Then Farmer Barnes hurried down the lane faster than ever.

'What next?' he said to himself.

'What next, you bad cow?' He went over the bridge by the pond, past two thatched cottages and along to the gates of Farmer Bailey's house. A big truck had stopped there to collect the milk. The driver was standing in the middle of the lane slowly shaking his head from side to side.

Farmer Barnes called out to him, 'Have you seen my Bluebell? She's run away and I cannot find her!'

'Don't bother me about *your* Bluebell,' said the driver, 'just look at *my* milk! I never saw such a mess in all my days!' The milk-cans were tumbled all over the lane and a pool of milk was trickling into the ditch.

'Dear me, what a business, what a mess!' said Farmer Barnes. 'Who would do that?' Farmer Barnes jumped over the cans and ran down the lane. Faster and faster he went.

He ran past the donkey field. He ran past Miss Smith's cottage. He ran into the village and down to the crossroads. He was puffing, so he stopped to take a deep breath.

He could not believe what he saw. The long road to market was full of cars and trucks. They stood in a line all the way to Thrush Bridge, and not one inch did they move. Farmer Barnes walked along to see what was the trouble. He saw a truck full of turnips, an old Ford, an army truck, Farmer Bailey in his station-wagon, the baker, two ice-cream men, three young men on motorcycles, and a cattle-truck. All the drivers scowled, and some blew their horns.

Thrush Bridge was a narrow bridge. When Farmer Barnes reached it he stopped, opened his eyes very wide, and said, '*Well!*'

In the middle of the bridge, sitting right across the road, peacefully chew-ing her cud, was . . . Bluebell!

She had flecks of milk on her ears.
Her nose was covered with squashed
plums. Apple-juice drooled from her
mouth. A piece of fencing stuck to one
horn; most of a lady's hat stuck to the
other horn. *And*, she was stopping all
the traffic and no-one could move her.

Farmer Barnes said, 'You are the silliest cow I ever saw! Come home, Bluebell!'

She got to her feet and stretched. She flicked her silky tail. She followed Farmer Barnes back down the road, and when they were in the lane he took out his big red handkerchief with white spots. He wiped Bluebell's nose, her mouth and her ears, until there was no trace of plums, or apples, or milk. He pulled the piece of fencing and part of a lady's hat off her horns.

On the way home they passed the driver, who was picking up his milk-cans. They saw Miss Smith, who waved from her cottage. They passed Mr Trench and his wife, who were scrubbing their table and sweeping up their plums. They passed Farmer Grey, who was mending his fence. Farmer Barnes said, 'Good day!' to them all, and gave Bluebell a smack to make her hurry home.

She flicked her tail. She licked her long red tongue round her nose. She gazed at them all with her soft brown eyes. She *looked* as good and quiet as a cow can be.

But Farmer Barnes knew better.

This story is by John Cunliffe.

The Sleepy-Mouse

Once upon a time, in the middle of a wood, lived a dormouse. He was more like a tiny squirrel than a mouse. He had big black eyes and fat furry ears and a thick, round, long, bushy tail.

Every summer he played in the trees, eating nuts and getting very fat. Then in the autumn, when he was plump and round, he would build a nest of moss and leaves, and put some nuts in it just for a snack. Then he would

cover his eyes,
and cover his nose,
and wrap his tail right over his toes.

Then he would wrap it over his back, and over his head, and use the tip of it for a pillow. And he would go to sleep for weeks and weeks.

The dormouse never knew which he liked best. Perhaps the light warm summer when he climbed up the trees after nuts and berries; then the sun made him so happy that sometimes, for a change, he would eat his dinner upside down, swinging from a branch by his toes. Or perhaps it was the winter he liked best, when he curled up in his soft warm nest and went to sleep; he would wake up now and then, if the weather was not too cold, and stay awake just long enough to eat a nut, then fall asleep again . . . Oh, it was a lovely life being a dormouse.

One April morning he woke up in his nest at the bottom of a hollow tree.

He uncovered his eyes,
he uncovered his nose,
he unwrapped the tail that covered
his toes.

75

He sat up and sniffed. How strange. It didn't smell like green grass and sunshine at all. It didn't smell like springtime. He wrinkled his nose. It was a *tickly* sort of smell. He peeped out of the tree – and nearly bumped his nose on an icicle.

Everything was white. His tree was covered with inches of snow at the top,

and buried in inches of snow at the bottom.

'I must have mistaken the date,' he said to himself. 'It can't be spring at all.' And he

covered his eyes,
and covered his nose,
and wrapped his tail right over his
toes.

And over his back, and over his head, and he used the tip of it for a pillow. But he couldn't get to sleep again.

'I'll just eat one nut,' he said to him-self. 'Then I'll fall asleep easily.' He reached out his paw for a nut, but there wasn't a nut there. He'd eaten them all up.

'Tickle my whiskers,' thought the

dormouse. 'I *never* eat all my nuts before spring-time.' He peeped out of the tree again, but it was just the same as before. Icicles hung like bars over his hole. And the snow was inches deep.

The dormouse sighed, for he was terribly hungry. He wasn't fat any more. He had grown thin during his long winter sleep, and he was ready to start eating again. But there was snow outside, and it couldn't be spring. So he

covered his eyes,
and covered his nose,
and wrapped his tail right over his
      toes.

And over his back and over his head, and he used the tip of it as a pillow. But he couldn't get to sleep. He was much too hungry. And he was cold. And if there is one thing that stops anyone from going to sleep, it is being hungry and cold.

He tossed and wriggled and hunched and snuggled, but it was no use at all. He would have to get up. So he

uncovered his eyes,
and uncovered his nose,
and uncurled the tail that covered his
toes.

And he peeped out of the tree. Brrh. It was freezing.

Very, very carefully the dormouse climbed along the snowy twigs. The snow stuck to his paws, and he had to shake them at every step.

There was nothing to be seen. No

leaves. No grass. No spring flowers. Nothing but the thick white snow.

He ran down the twig again and on to the ground. What was a dormouse to do? His claws made patterns on the snow, as he ran this way and that, poking his nose into the thickets, hoping to find just a little snack to eat. But there was nothing, nothing at all. The dormouse was so tired with searching, that he squeezed into the hedge, and he decided that after a little rest, he would look again.

While the dormouse was lying curled up in the hedge, some children came running along. They wore thick coats and leggings, woolly hats and wellingtons. Soon they started a snow fight, and one of the snowballs hit the hedge and made the dormouse jump. He poked his head out, wondering whatever was happening.

'Oh, a sleepy-mouse, a sleepy-mouse,' cried the children. And one little girl quickly picked up the dormouse. He was so cold and frozen, he didn't try to run away. The little girl put him inside her coat.

What a wonderful thing! All the snow that was clinging to his fur melted, and he began to feel warm again. He shook his whiskers, and curled himself up, next to her jersey. Then he

covered his eyes,
and covered his nose,
and wrapped his tail right over his
    toes.

And when the children reached school, the dormouse was fast asleep.

In the classroom the little girl ran up to the teacher. 'I've brought a sleepy-mouse, a sleepy-mouse,' she cried. And very, very gently she unbuttoned her coat and showed the little dormouse still fast asleep, his paws over his face.

'Was he sleeping like this when you found him? Or was he wide awake, ready for spring?' asked the teacher.

'Oh, he was awake, looking very surprised at the snow.'

'I expect he can't understand why the sun isn't shining when April's already here. He has woken up to have his first spring breakfast, and his breakfast is buried in the snow. That's what happens when we have a very bad winter. Poor little dormouse. We'll have to find something for him here instead.'

The children gathered round, while the teacher put some cottonwool in a box, and brought a handful of corn and

a saucer of water. The dormouse woke up, shook his whiskers, and settled down to breakfast. When he had finished, he lay down in the box, and

covered his eyes,
and covered his nose,
and wrapped his tail right over his toes.

And he went to sleep. He stayed with the children for two weeks, until the thaw came and the snow melted. Then one day the children took him out into the field where they had found him. The sun was shining. The grass was green. And the late bluebells were opening their petals.

'Goodbye, dormouse,' they said. 'Now you can look after yourself.' And they watched him as he scampered over the grass and up the twigs of a beech tree. 'Goodbye,' they shouted. 'Goodbye, sleepy-mouse.' Then they ran back to school, for it was lesson-time again.

This story is by Leila Berg.

The Weather Cat

John was upstairs helping his mother to make beds. Downstairs they heard a noise.

'There's someone downstairs,' said John. 'In the kitchen.'

'Go down and see,' his mother said. 'It will be Mr Briggs. Ask him to wait, please.'

John went downstairs and into the kitchen. There, rolling a reel of cotton

across the floor, was a small tabby cat. John looked at the cat. The cat looked back at John.

'Good morning, Mr Briggs,' said John. 'Mother says please will you wait?'

The tabby cat went back to its game, and the cotton reel went to and fro. Then John gave it a kick. The cat liked that. His tail twitched. He crouched and sprang.

John's mother came in. 'What's this?' she said.

'Mr Briggs and I are having a game of football,' John told her. 'He's good at it.'

'That's not Mr Briggs!' she cried.

'Yes it is,' John told her. 'Another Mr Briggs.'

John fetched a jug and a saucer. 'Would you like some milk, Mr Briggs?' he asked. 'It's half-time.'

The cat purred. 'You see,' said John, 'it *is* his name.'

Just then the real Mr Briggs came in. He had come to put in a new window-pane. 'What's this?' he asked. 'I didn't know you had a cat.'

'We didn't have one yesterday,' John said, 'but today we have. His name is Mr Briggs. Same as you.'

'Fancy that!' said Mr Briggs.

At dinner-time one Mr Briggs went

home. The other stayed and ate fish-tails and drank two saucers of milk. You can guess which did which.

One Mr Briggs stayed all afternoon. He curled himself up on the window-sill.

'Can he stay?' John asked. 'I think he likes it here.'

'If he had a home, he would go there,' said his mother. 'He can stay if he likes.'

Mr Briggs did like.

And next day John found a white plate and a white dish. Round the rims he painted MR BRIGGS in red paint. Now Mr Briggs really had come to stay.

Every morning John came down to let him out. Mr Briggs would drink a saucer of milk and then go out into the garden.

After a week or two, John began to notice something.

If it was fine, Mr Briggs would go and lie on top of the shed. He was looking for birds.

If it was fine but cold, he would lie inside the shed. He lay very still behind the plant pots. He was looking for mice.

But if it was wet, Mr Briggs would soon come back into the house. He came on tip-toe, so as not to get his feet wet. Then he went into the cupboard under the stairs and slept all morning.

Then John noticed something else.

On some days, Mr Briggs would come and lie in his cupboard even when it was fine. On the days when he did that, it always *did* rain, later on.

'Mr Briggs is a weather cat!' John told his mother. 'He always knows when it's going to rain!'

His mother was hanging out the washing. 'It isn't going to rain today,' she said.

'Yes it is!' said John. 'Mr Briggs is under the stairs!'

His mother laughed and went back inside. Not long after it began to rain. It poured. John and his mother ran out to take in the washing.

'I told you!' John cried. 'Mr Briggs is a weather cat!'

After than everyone took notice of what Mr Briggs did.

'He's on top of the shed today,' John's father would say. 'No need to take my

umbrella.' Or, 'He's inside the shed –
I'd better take my overcoat!'

John's mother would wait to see what
Mr Briggs did every morning. If he lay
on top of the shed she would have a
wash day. But if he went into his cupboard she would say, 'Better wait until
tomorrow. Mr Briggs is under the
stairs.'

One very fine day Mr Briggs went
under the stairs.

'That's funny,' John said. 'It doesn't
look a bit like rain.'

'I shan't wash today,' said his mother. 'Mr Briggs is never wrong.'

At dinner-time Mr Briggs was still in his cupboard. And there hadn't been one drop of rain. Not a single drop.

John went and looked under the stairs. There lay Mr Briggs, looking up at him. And there, at his side, lay one, two, three, four little—

'Mother!' yelled John. 'Come and look.'

She ran from the kitchen and looked in the cupboard.

Now the tabby cat is called Mrs Briggs and has four weather kittens.

On fine days they lie on the roof of the shed, looking for birds.

On cold days they lie inside the shed, looking for mice.

And on wet days, they sleep in the cupboard under the stairs.

Soon John will be giving the kittens away. Does anyone want a weather cat?

This story is by Helen Cresswell.

Poonam's Pets

Poonam is in Class One and her teacher is Mrs Wig.

Poonam is a bit on the small side and a bit on the quiet side. In fact you have to put your ear right down by her mouth if you want to hear what she is saying.

'All right, Class One,' said Mrs Wig one day. 'Be quiet and listen. I've got something special to tell you. On

Friday,' said Mrs Wig, 'we are going to have a Pets Assembly. That means you can bring your pets to school, and they can go to Assembly.' Everybody laughed. It was funny to think of pets in Assembly. 'Now,' said Mrs Wig, 'how many of you have got pets?' Everyone in Class One put up their hands.

'That's a lot of pets,' said Mrs Wig. 'Let's see what sort of pets we have.'

There were dogs and cats and goldfish and rabbits. Ranjeev put his hand up for everything, but Poonam didn't put her hand up at all.

'All right,' said Mrs Wig, 'have any of you got . . . *giraffes*?'

Only Ranjeev put his hand up.

'Ranjeev,' said Mrs Wig. 'You can't have a *giraffe*!'

'I have,' said Ranjeev. 'He's got big brown spots.'

'Poonam,' said Mrs Wig. 'You haven't said anything yet. What sort of pet have you got?'

Poonam got up very quietly and walked to Mrs Wig's table, and Mrs Wig put her ear down, and Poonam whispered into it.

'Poonam's got *lions*,' said Mrs Wig to Class One. Poonam smiled a quiet little smile.

On Friday, all the pets came to the Pets Assembly. Some of them came in cars, some came in boxes, some came in hutches, and some came in cages. Kamaljit's dog came in a pram, because he was an old dog. All the other dogs walked to school on leads.

The goldfish were very quiet and good. The cats were *quite* well behaved, except for one or two who were

making horrible faces at the dogs and spitting at them. Julie's dog Prince wanted to sniff everyone's trousers, and Gurpal's dog Pongo barked all the time and wanted to fight everybody.

'I'm not sure if this Pets Assembly is such a good idea, after all,' said Mrs Wig.

Ranjeev came a little bit late, and rather out of puff. He had a big bulge under his jumper.

'What's in there, Ranjeev?' said Gurpal.

'My giraffe,' said Ranjeev.

'Looks more like a rabbit to me,' said Gurpal.

'It's a giraffe!' shouted Ranjeev. 'It's just not grown up yet!'

'I think my dog Pongo would like to eat your giraffe,' said Gurpal.

It was nearly time for Assembly, and everyone in Class One was there except Poonam. Mrs Wig looked at the clock.

'Well,' said Mrs Wig. 'I'm afraid we'll have to start. Line up quietly please, dogs on the left and cats on the right.' Lining up took quite a long time because some of the dogs got mixed up. Dogs are not very good at telling left from right. And then they all went into the hall.

The hall looked beautiful, with the dogs on one side and the cats on the other side. It did not matter where the goldfish sat, because goldfish are very peaceful.

When they saw all the other children looking at their pets, the children in Class One felt very pleased and proud.

And still Poonam had not come.

Mrs Wig went to the front of the hall. 'Good morning, everybody,' she said. 'Welcome to Class One's Special Pets Assembly.'

And then something amazing happened. The door opened, and in came Poonam. And behind Poonam, walking very quietly, one behind the other in a row, were . . .

. . . SIX ENORMOUS LIONS!

All the dogs got under the chairs. The cats opened their eyes wide and stared. They had never seen such big cats before.

Ranjeev's giraffe was very frightened, and burrowed deep under his

jumper. The children were frightened
as well, and wanted to run out.

Poonam and her six enormous lions
walked right to the front of the hall, and
the lions sat down in a row, blinking
sleepily at the children. They did not
look too fierce. They looked solemn
and friendly and wise.

105

Poonam went up to Mrs Wig. Mrs Wig bent her ear down and Poonam whispered in it. Then Mrs Wig stood up straight. 'Poonam says we are not to be frightened,' she said. 'These are very good lions.' Poonam whispered in Mrs Wig's ear again. 'Poonam says her lions will now do their act for you,' said Mrs Wig.

Poonam clapped her hands. Two lions balanced their front paws on chairs while the lions behind stood up on their back legs, balancing with their paws on each other's shoulders. They all opened their mouths wide, showing their huge teeth, and Poonam gave each of them a big lion biscuit. All the children clapped and cheered. The lions sat down in a row again, looking very pleased with themselves.

Poonam whispered to Mrs Wig.

'Ask them yourself, Poonam,' said Mrs Wig.

Poonam turned and looked at the children. Then she said in a very loud voice: 'WOULD ANYBODY LIKE A RIDE ON MY LIONS?'

The children were amazed. No-one had ever heard Poonam speak with a loud voice before.

So the whole school went out to the playground and the six enormous lions stood in a row. They were very big, but Poonam and Mrs Wig helped the little ones to get up.

But when it was Ranjeev's turn he stood and looked at the ground.

'What's the matter, Ranjeev?' said Poonam. Ranjeev whispered in Poonam's ear. 'What?' said Poonam.

'I can't hear you.'

'I'm a bit scared,' said Ranjeev.

'It's all right,' said Poonam. 'I'll hold your hand.'

Poonam and the six enormous lions stayed all day. When it was home time, she clapped her hands to the lions. They lined up and Poonam and her six enormous lions went quietly home.

*

Poonam is still a bit small, and rather quiet. But when she has something important to say, she says it with a loud voice. She never talks about her six enormous lions, and no-one has ever seen them since the day of the Pets Assembly.

This story is by Andrew and Diana Davies.

How Grandfather Found
His Voice

On Tuesday afternoon, Grandfather
met Rosa from school and took her
home with him for tea. He did this
every Tuesday and Thursday without
fail, because on those two days Rosa's
mother worked in a hospital and wasn't
home in time to meet her. Rosa didn't
have a father. As far as she could remember, she'd never had a father.

'I've got something special to show

you today,' said Grandfather as they walked hand in hand to his small, ground–floor flat.

'What is it, Grandad? What is it?'

'I'm not telling. But it's got four legs and whiskers.'

'I know, I know,' said Rosa, dancing with excitement. 'It's kittens. Your Polly's had kittens. Polly's had kittens,' she sang. 'Polly's had kittens.'

'Just one kitten,' said Grandfather. 'Well, just one kitten now, anyway. Poor little mite.'

When they got to Grandfather's flat, Rosa rushed in shouting: 'Where is it? Where is it? I want to see it.'

'It's not an it,' said Grandfather. 'She's a she. And she's in the broom cupboard.'

And so she was, a tiny, furry, grey bundle in a shoe box, snuggling against her mother. She was so small and fast asleep that Rosa hardly dared breathe or move or make a sound.

'What are you going to call her, Grandad?' she whispered.

'Don't know,' said Grandad. 'What do you think she looks like?'

'Gravy,' said Rosa. 'Can we call her Gravy?'

Grandfather led Rosa into the kitchen. 'Gravy, Gravy, give me your answer, do,' he sang. 'Well, why not? We'll call her Gravy and see how she likes it. Come on, now. Boiled eggs for tea.'

'I can boil eggs,' said Rosa.

'You just lay the table,' said Grandad. 'I'm in charge here.'

So Rosa put the plates and the tea-spoons and the egg-cups on the table

113

while Grandfather carefully pricked a hole at the end of each egg with a pin before he put them in boiling water. He sliced the brown bread and buttered it and cut up some tomato and cucumber, and put the special cakes he'd bought on his large old plate, which was decorated with pink roses. And all the

while, he was singing to himself, 'Daisy, Daisy, give me your answer, do—'

'Why are you always singing, Grandad?' asked Rosa.

'Doesn't your mum sing?' asked Grandad.

'Sometimes,' said Rosa. 'When she's in a good mood. Not always.'

'Well,' said Grandfather as they sat down to have their tea, 'do you know how many brothers and sisters I had?'

Rosa thought. 'Five,' she said at last.

'More,' said Grandad.

'Fifteen,' said Rosa.

'Four brothers and three sisters,' said Grandad. 'How many does that make?'

'Seven,' said Rosa.

'Quite right. And with all those children, do you think anyone took any notice of a little pipsqueak like me?'

'No,' said Rosa.

'Not a blind bit of notice,' Grandad went on. 'Until—' Then he stopped and stared at Rosa as if he'd forgotten what he was saying.

'Until what?' asked Rosa.

'You just eat your tea and stop asking questions,' said Grandad. 'Otherwise, all your teeth might fall out. See these,' he said, opening his mouth. 'All mine. Seventy-eight and all my own teeth. Well, nearly. That's because when I was your age, I never asked questions.'

Rosa looked at him to see if he was joking. He had a toothy grin, so she laughed.

'Wouldn't have made any difference if I had asked questions,' said Grand-father. 'No-one ever listened to me. Until one Friday, I was having my

116

weekly bath in front of the fire in the kitchen. We didn't have a proper bath, of course, no taps with running hot and cold water and that sort of thing. And no-one was taking any notice of me as usual. And the water was getting colder and colder. So I said, just to see what would happen, I said, as loud as I could, "I can sing a song".'

'What did happen?' asked Rosa.

'Not much,' said Grandfather. 'All my brothers and sisters were fighting and playing and my mum was making supper and my dad poked his head over his paper and said, "Did you hear what the little lad said?" He always called me the little lad because he couldn't remember my name. And my mum went on cooking and my brothers and sisters went on playing and fighting and

my dad went on reading the paper.

'So I thought, I'll show them. And I opened my mouth and out came this voice I never knew I had. That did it. They were all amazed. They stopped what they were doing and gathered round the bath-tub and listened to me sing. Afterwards my dad asked for three cheers for the little lad.'

Rosa clapped her hands excitedly. 'What song did you sing?' she asked.

'It's funny you should ask that,' he said, 'because I remember it as if it was yesterday. It was the one about the kipper.'

And he opened his arms and mouth wide and sang:

'*You should hold a kipper in one hand not two*
And wave it while you're talking like the big shots do.
Never put your elbows on the table while you eat
But leave a little room for other folks to park their feet . . .'

119

Rosa joined in at the end because she'd heard the song hundreds of times before.

'You'd better have the last cake, Rosa,' said Grandad.

'Can I?' she said.

'Since you've asked so nicely,' he said, 'you might as well.' So she did.

'After that,' Grandad said, 'they took notice of me all right. They called me the little lad with the voice. And that's how I got where I am today,' he said, laughing.

Later that evening, Rosa was in her own kitchen, watching her mother wash up the crockery left over from breakfast.

'Mum,' said Rosa.

Rosa's mum didn't say anything, because she was thinking about what they were going to have for dinner the next day.

'Mum,' said Rosa again.

'Isn't it time you went to bed?' said her mother as she dried her hands.

'Can I have a bath?' asked Rosa.

'What, now?' said her mother. 'I must sew this button on your dress and then there's a programme I want to watch on the telly. Anyway, it's too late now and you had a bath yesterday.'

And she started to thread the needle to sew the button on Rosa's dress.

'Mum,' said Rosa.

'Rosa,' said her mum, 'I thought I told you to get ready for bed.'

'I can sing a song,' said Rosa.

'I'm sure you can,' said her mother absent-mindedly.

Rosa stood up and opened her arms

and her mouth and began to sing:

'You should hold a kipper in one hand not two
And wave it while you're talking like the big shots do——'

Her mother looked at Rosa as she sang, and when it came to the last line she joined in because she'd heard the song hundreds of times before.

'I haven't heard that in a long time,' said Rosa's mother. Then suddenly she put down her sewing and picked up Rosa and kissed her.

'I do know you're here,' she said to Rosa. 'Even when I'm busy doing other things, I haven't forgotten you. How could I do that?' she said.

And she gave her a big hug.

This story is by Leon Rosselson.

Pappa's Going to Buy You a
Mocking Bird

Once there was a girl called Belinda, but her pappa called her Honeybee. Every night, when he came home from the coalmine, he sang her a goodnight song.

Who looked after Belinda in the day-time? Her granny.

Where was her mum? In hospital. But she would be home soon.

One night, Belinda's pa came home

from work. 'What was it like in the mine today, Pappa?'

'Dark, my honeybęe. Dark and noisy. Things go thump and things go clang. And the coal trundles along on the trolley.'

Belinda looked at the coal burning away in the fire, red and bright. She thought about how it would look rolling along on a trolley – like a necklace of red beads.

Then her pa took her on his knee and he sang:

'*Hush, my honeybee, don't say a word,*
Pappa's going to buy you a mocking
    bird . . .'

Then off skipped Belinda, upstairs to bed in her cornery little bedroom with its window that looked over the steep valley and away across the river to the other mountain.

She went straight to sleep. And she began to dream. She dreamed that her pappa gave her a beautiful grey and white bird, tame and friendly as a person, that would sit on her shoulder, or perch on the top of her head, and take a cherry or a cake-crumb from her fingers.

But would that bird sing?

Not a note! Not a single note!

'Please, please sing to me, Mocking Bird!' said Belinda.

But the mocking bird shook its head.

Then, with a flip and a waft of its wings, it flew away from Belinda, down the hill, across the brook at the bottom, and up the other side on to the distant mountain.

There sat a boy on a rock, watching. He put out his arm sideways, like a sign-post. And the mocking bird flew up the hill to him and perched on his wrist. Then, far, far away in the distance, Belinda could hear it begin to sing.

Oh, how it sang! It twittered and rippled, it chirruped, it chuckled and cheeped, whistled and fluted, warbled, carolled, lilted, quavered, trilled, and thrilled.

Why should it sing to that boy and not to me? Belinda wondered sadly.

Next night, when her pa came home from the mine, she asked him, 'What was it like in the mine today, Pa?'

'Dark, my honeybee,' he said. 'Dark and hot. And the coal went rumble-rumble-rumble.'

Belinda looked at the coal burning red in the fire. She thought about how it would be if it had a loud voice and rumbled.

Her pa took her on his knee, and he sang:

'*Hush, my honeybee, don't say a word,*
Pappa's going to buy you a mocking bird;
And if that mocking bird won't sing
Pappa's going to buy you a diamond ring.'

Off went Belinda to bed in her little room that looked out, away, away, over the grassy valley to the other mountain. And she went to sleep.

She dreamed that her pappa gave her a silver ring with a big shiny diamond on it, glossy as a cherry. But the ring didn't fit – she could hardly squeeze it on her littlest finger. She tried and tried, pushed and pushed, but it wouldn't go on. Then, while she stood holding the ring between finger and thumb, the mocking bird came sailing across the valley on his grey and white wings, and

129

gently took the ring from her in his beak. Away he flew again, over the brook at the bottom and up the other side. And there sat the boy on his rock – too far off for Belinda to see his face.

The mocking bird carried the ring to him, and he slid it on to his finger.

'Oh!' cried Belinda in a rage. 'That's not fair!'

That woke her up – and she found it was morning.

In the evening, when her pa came home from work, she asked him, 'What was it like in the mine today, Pappa?'

'Dark, my honeybee,' her pappa said, ruffling her hair. 'And hot. And the wheels whirred. And the coal crashed and scrunched.'

Belinda looked at the red coal in the fire, and wondered what it would sound like if it began to crash and scrunch.

Then her pa took her on his knee, and he sang:

'Hush, my honeybee, don't say a word,
Pappa's going to buy you a mocking bird.
And if that mocking bird won't sing
Pappa's going to buy you a diamond ring.
And if that diamond ring's too small
Pappa's going to buy you a sky-blue ball.'

Off went Belinda to bed, in her little room high up over the valley. The window was full of stars tonight. She lay awake looking at the stars for all of three minutes before she went to sleep.

She dreamed that her pappa gave her a beautiful blue ball, covered with golden stars. She tossed it and she caught it, she rolled it and she bounced

it, she threw it high in the air and then
it came swooping back into her cupped
hands. But after she had tossed and
caught it a dozen times, the sky-blue
ball suddenly slipped out of her clasped
hands, and began to roll away down the
hill. Faster and faster it rolled – until it
looked like a blue streak with golden

lines along its sides. Over the bridge at the bottom it bounced – and the boy on the far hillside jumped up from his rock, and ran down and caught it.

Then he waved, and called something to Belinda, but what he called she could not hear.

'You give me back my ball!' shouted Belinda, so loudly that she woke herself up, and it was morning.

When her pa came home from work that night she asked him, 'What was it like down there today, Pappa?'

'Dark and hot and dirty, my honeybee. Dark and hot and noisy. But never mind: tomorrow's Saturday, and Mama's coming home with a surprise for us.'

And he took Belinda on his knee and sang:

'Hush, my honeybee, don't say a word,
Pappa's going to buy you a mocking bird.
And if that mocking bird won't sing
Pappa's going to buy you a diamond ring.
And if that diamond ring's too small
Pappa's going to buy you a sky-blue ball.
And if that ball should chance to flee
You're still Pappa's little honeybee!'

Then he hugged Belinda and she went off to bed in her little high-up room that looked out over the valley. And, in a corner of the room, there was a new small bed that had not been there before. Belinda looked at it and wondered about it for all of two minutes before she went off to sleep.

And that night, in her dream, the boy across the valley threw back the sky-blue ball, and it came bounding and

bouncing up the hill and settled in her hands. He sent back the mocking bird carrying the ring. Belinda put the ring on her finger, and it slid right on. And the mocking bird sang and sang, all night, most beautifully.

'Why don't you come too?' Belinda called to the boy. 'Across the valley, to hear the bird sing?'

But he shook his head.

'What's your name?' she called.

'My name's Tom!' he called faintly across the wide distance of the valley. And he added something else that Belinda could not quite hear.

Next day Belinda's pappa stayed at home because it was Saturday. And he helped Belinda and her granny get the house all clean and polished and shining, with primroses and violets from the garden in every empty jam-pot.

And that afternoon Belinda's mother came home from the hospital with a new baby.

'There!' said Belinda's granny. 'He's a lovely boy! He'll be a playmate for you, by and by.'

'What's his name?' asked Belinda.

'We thought you'd like to choose it,' said her mother. 'He isn't named yet.'

Belinda thought for a long time. Then she said, 'Could his name be Tom?'

This story is by Joan Aiken.

Acknowledgements

The editor and publisher are grateful for permission to include the following copyright material in this anthology:

Joan Aiken, 'Pappa's Going to Buy You a Mocking Bird'. From *Past Eight O'Clock*. First published by Jonathan Cape. Copyright © Joan Aiken, 1986. Reprinted by permission of A M Heath & Co Ltd.

Ruth Ainsworth, 'The Bear who Liked Hugging People'. First published by William Heinemann. Copyright © Ruth Ainsworth, 1966. Reprinted by permission of Reed Consumer Books Ltd.

Leila Berg, 'The Sleepy-Mouse' from *Lollipops*. Copyright © Leila Berg. Reprinted by permission of Hodder & Stoughton Ltd.

Helen Cresswell, 'The Weather Cat'. First published by Ernest Benn Ltd. Copyright © Helen Cresswell, 1989. Reprinted by permission of HarperCollins Publishers.

John Cunliffe, 'Farmer Barnes and Bluebell'. First published by André Deutsch. Copyright © John Cunliffe. Reprinted by permission of David Higham Associates Ltd.

Andrew and Diana Davies, 'Poonam's Pets'. First published by Methuen. Copyright © Andrew and Diana Davies, 1990. Reprinted by permission of Reed Consumer Books Ltd.

June Epstein, ' Alexander', from *Family Treasures and other Bedtime Stories* ed. Rosalind Price and Walter McVitty. Copyright © June Epstein, 1987.

Wendy Eyton, 'The Magic Thistledown Dog', from *Tales from the Threepenny Bit*. Copyright © Wendy Eyton, 1990. Reprinted by permission of HarperCollins Publishers.

Ruth Manning-Sanders, 'Yanni', from *A Book of Dragons*. First published by Methuen. Copyright © Ruth Manning-Sanders, 1964. Reprinted by permission of David Higham Associates Ltd.

Leon Rosselson, 'How Grandfather Found His Voice', from *Rosa's Singing Grandfather*. Copyright © Leon Rosselson, 1991. First published by Viking in 1991 and in Puffin Books in 1992.

Catherine Storr, 'Tom', from *Pob's Stories*, ed. by Anne Wood. First published by Fontana. Copyright © Catherine Storr, 1985. Reprinted by permission of the author.

Every effort has been made to trace and contact copyright holders before publication. If any errors or omissions occur, the publisher will be pleased to rectify these at the earliest opportunity.